MW00962708

This edition published in 1990 by Gallery Books,
an imprint of W.H. Smith Publishers, Inc.
112 Madison Avenue, New York, New York 10016

Produced for Gallery Books by Joshua Morris Publishing, Inc.,
221 Danbury Road, Wilton, CT 06897

Gallery Books are available for bulk purchase
for sales promotions and premium use.
For details write or telephone the Manager of Special Sales,
W.H. Smith Publishers, Inc., 112 Madison Avenue,
New York, New York 10016   (212) 532-6600.

Sleepytime Tales

Written by Marcia Perry
Illustrated by Yuri Saltzman

GALLERY BOOKS
An Imprint of W. H. Smith Publishers Inc.
112 Madison Avenue
New York City 10016

The Rabbit, Squirrel, and Otter families happily sat around the campfire on the first night of their three-day camping trip. Young Pearl Squirrel, Olly Otter, and Ruby Rabbit watched the stars come out overhead.

"It's time all junior campers were asleep," announced Uncle Otter.

"But you promised to tell us a story every night," said Ruby.

"So I did, Ruby," said Uncle Otter. "Since you reminded me, I'll make up this first one about you. It's called..."

RUBY RABBIT LOGS A VICTORY

Ruby Rabbit was hurrying through the woods carrying a basket with a jar of hot soup in it for sick Gertie Groundhog. Suddenly from behind a huckleberry bush pounced fat old Franklin Fox.

"EEEEK!" squealed Ruby. "EEEEEK!"

"Stop shrieking!" barked Franklin. "You're hurting my ears!" He stopped short and covered his ears with his paws.

In that instant, Ruby hopped at top speed into a hollow log.

Franklin poked his nose into the log. "Mighty fine-smelling soup you've got there. Give it to me and hop along home."

Ruby quickly thought of a way to try and fool Franklin.

"I can't, Mr. Fox!" fibbed Ruby. "If only I weren't so plump, I could. But I'm stuck!"

Hearing this, sly old Franklin slunk around to the other end of the log.

"From this end, I can easily snatch the soup from that fat bunny!" he chuckled and leaped headlong into the log.

But instead of finding the soup, Franklin found himself stuck fast in the narrow log. And where was Ruby? She had hopped out of the log!

"I fooled you, Mr. Fox," laughed Ruby. "I hope you'll excuse me if I don't help you," she called. "But I can't let my soup get cold."

And with that, she scampered off to visit Gertie Groundhog, who said she had never tasted such good, hot soup.

R uby, Olly, and Pearl enjoyed Uncle Otter's first-night story so much that on the second night, they were in their sleeping bags ready for bed even before the moon was up over the oak trees.

"Uncle Otter," asked Pearl Squirrel, "what story are you going to tell us tonight?"

"One for you, Pearl!" Uncle Otter replied. "It's called…"

PEARL SQUIRREL AND THE MISSING WALNUTS

Aunt Fluffy had forgotten where her walnuts were buried. "Gracious me!" she exclaimed, "I've got company coming and no walnuts! I'd give a whole pie to whomever could find them."

"I'll find them for you!" said Pearl Squirrel.

Pearl Squirrel ran to where Aunt Fluffy thought the walnuts might be buried. But Farmer Carter's dog, Peabody was already there.

Barking and howling, Peabody ran toward Pearl, who quickly scrambled up a tree.

"Hush up!" Pearl scolded.

"I won't!" snarled Peabody. "You're just the little squirrel I want for some squirrel stew."

"If you'll leave me alone, I'll show you where a wonderful dinner is buried," Pearl said.

The thought of a beefy bone filled Peabody's head.

"It's a deal," he growled. "Where do I dig?"

Pearl pointed to a mossy mound. "There!" said
Pearl.

Peabody dug and dug. Dirt flew out from
between his hind legs, but that was all.

"There's nothing in this hole but dirt," growled Peabody at last.

"Maybe I made a mistake," said Pearl. "Dig over by that log."

Again Peabody's big paws set to work. Rocks flew out from between his legs, but that was all.

"There's nothing in this hole but rocks!" Peabody snapped.

"Well, try digging between the roots of that beech tree," Pearl suggested.

Peabody started digging again. This time, oodles and oodles of walnuts came flying up!

"There isn't any bone in this hole either!"
Peabody sighed, all tuckered out. "And now I hear
Farmer Carter calling me. I haven't even got time
to chase you! Goodbye for now."

Pearl laughed and called after him, "Thanks for
digging up a wonderful dinner, Peabody! Dinner
for us squirrels, that is!"

Pearl collected all the walnuts Peabody had dug
up and delivered them to Aunt Fluffy for her pies.
And Pearl ate the biggest pie all by herself!

On the last night of the trip, Ruby Rabbit, Pearl Squirrel, and Olly Otter were allowed to stay up very late to watch the meteor showers. They were all bundled up in their sleeping bags, staring up at the sky.

"Uncle Otter," asked Olly, yawning, "could you make up a story about me?"

So Uncle Otter told the story about…

HOW SILLINESS SAVED
OLLY OTTER

Olly Otter was on his way to his favorite
riverbank slide. Suddenly Wally Wolf leaped out
from behind a tree and grabbed his tail.

"Gotcha!" Wally cried. "Just try and get away!"

But Olly didn't move. He just smiled and rolled
over on his back.

"Thank goodness you came along, Wally," Olly
said. "You can put an end to my troubles."

"Troubles? What's wrong?" asked the wolf.

"I've just come from Doctor Owl's. He says..." Olly started to cry.

"You're sick, aren't you?" asked Wally Wolf.

Gravely, Olly answered, "He said I had the most serious case of the sillies that he'd ever seen!" Olly burst out crying again.

"What does it feel like to have the sillies?" Wally asked nervously.

"Owww!" yelled Olly, as he twisted into a ball and flipped himself over.

"Yeoww!" he groaned, somersaulting back and collapsing again.

"It makes your sides ache," Olly murmured. "Then, it makes you cry."

"How do you catch the sillies?" asked Wally anxiously, backing away from the otter.

"You catch it from something that already has it. It must have been that fish I ate for lunch," Olly sobbed.

"Please, Mr. Wolf, gobble me up and end my misery!" Olly said, closing his eyes.

But all was silent. Olly opened one eye, then the other. The wolf had vanished!

Olly jumpcd up and started to laugh. He laughed and laughed till his side began to ache. Olly laughed until tears streamed down his face— but they weren't sad tears at all. They were glad tears that he had tricked Wally Wolf into letting him go free!